To my sweet son who still finds comfort in the arms of his Dear Mama.
To my husband who not only supports, but also encourages my wildest dreams.
– C.K.

For Mama, who sacrificed her own happiness for mine. I love you.
– S.C.

ISBN 978-1-953859-00-6 (Hardcover)
ISBN 978-1-953859-01-3 (E-Book)

Library of Congress Control Number: 2020919175
Printed in China

Text by Ceece Kelley
Illustrations by Sawyer Cloud
Book design by Tobi Carter
Edited by Nadara "Nay" Merrill

First edition 2020.

Soaring Kite Books
Washington, D.C.
United States of America
www.soaringkitebooks.com

Dear Mama's Loving Arms

written by
Ceece Kelley

illustrated by
Sawyer Cloud

The morning sun crawls through
my nursery room window.

A new day is here!

It’s time to be in Dear Mama’s
loving arms again.

Where is my giraffe pal? I lift up my sleep sack to look for him.

"Oh, there you are, Raffie.

I thought you ran away while I was sleeping." Raffie's arm is stitched from where I chewed it, but I love him anyway.

I hear Dear Mama's footsteps
on the creaky floor.

I **KICK** my legs with excitement.

I miss being in her arms when I sleep.

Dear Mama whisks me out of my crib and into her loving arms. Will she sing our special song? Yes! Here it comes...

Who loves Baby the most?

Who hugs Baby the most?
Who kisses Baby the most?
Your Dear Mama - that's who.

She sings and tickles and
smothers me in kisses.
I giggle and smile at her happily in return.

We laugh and play all day-

but I'm even happier when

Dear Mama

holds me in her

loving arms again.

My tummy lets out a **BIG rumble**.
Dear Mama knows what this means!
Before I know it, I'm in my high chair.

My milk makes my tummy warm, and my veggies make my tummy full. I slowly lean over and close my eyes. But I catch myself and blink my eyes awake!

"Who's a sleepy baby?" Dear Mama teases.

Not me! I do not want to nap!

She **scoops** me up into her soothing arms.

Dear Mama hums our special song
and sways me side to side.

Oh no!

I know exactly what comes next.
I smile sweetly and bat my long lashes.

No nap, Dear Mama!

But nap time is calling me.

I hear Dear Mama's footsteps on the creaky floor.
I lift my head up from her chest and clutch harder onto her arms.

Oh no! She's taking me to my room!

I FUSS and I FIGHT, and I FLAIL my arms all around. She starts to lay me down, so I let out a **BIG** wail.

No nap time for me!

Dear Mama strokes my curls with her fingers, and
makes shushing sounds against my forehead.
Then she lays me down all the way.

Dear Mama places Raffie near my face,
and his soft fur brushes against my cheek.
I squint to keep my eyes open.
I won't close my eyes.
Well, maybe just a little.

YAWN.

I can't hold out any longer.

I can't be in Dear Mama's
arms right now.
But maybe Dear Mama
can be in my *dreams*...

MOM

A warm kiss is placed on my forehead. I slowly open my eyes.
I'm rocking back and forth in Dear Mama's loving arms.
She squeezes me tight and sings,

Who loves Baby the most?
Who hugs Baby the most?
Who missed Baby the most?
Your Dear Mama - that's who.